W9-BRZ-278

Sp83t

THEY'RE
ALL NAMED
WILDFIRE

BOOKS BY NANCY SPRINGER

Not on a White Horse
They're All Named Wildfire

THEY'RE ALL NAMED
WILDFIRE
Nancy Springer

Atheneum

1989

NEW YORK

RETA E. KING LIBRARY
CHADRON STATE COLLEGE
CHADRON, NE 69337

Copyright © 1989 by Nancy Springer
All rights reserved. No part of this book may be reproduced
or transmitted in any form or by any means, electronic or
mechanical, including photocopying, recording, or by any
information storage and retrieval system, without permission
in writing from the publisher.

Atheneum
Macmillan Publishing Company
866 Third Avenue, New York, NY 10022
Collier Macmillan Canada, Inc.

First Edition   Printed in the United States of America
1 2 3 4 5 6 7 8 9 10

Library of Congress Cataloging-in-Publication Data
Springer, Nancy.
They're all named Wildfire/by Nancy Springer
—1st ed. p. cm.
Summary: Jenny loses most of her friends and suffers the verbal
abuse of classmates when she befriends a black girl who has moved
with her family into Jenny's duplex and shares her interest in horses.
ISBN 0-689-31450-7
[1. Prejudices—Fiction. 2. Race relations—Fiction.
3. Friendship—Fiction. 4. Horses—Fiction. 5. Afro-Americans—
Fiction.] I. Title. II. Title: They're all named Wildfire.
PZ7.S76846Th 1989 [Fic]—dc19 88-27497 CIP AC

To Nora,
who someday will have a horse of her
own

Gift (11.95)

Macmillan

4-18-89

+
Sp83t

THEY'RE
ALL NAMED
WILDFIRE

One

ME, I'm just a regular kid. My name's Jenny.
I've got blond hair turning brown, sort of blue-
brown eyes, freckles, sunburn, same as everybody else. But Shanterey was different.

She was real tall, for one thing. She looked
like she was put together out of long iron pipes
with long, flat muscles on them. And she was real
quiet. I never heard her giggle. It was like she
was a lot older than me, even though she was the
same age. She always seemed to be thinking.
And she wore braids in her hair. But that wasn't
what made her different. She was black.

And in my town black is about as different
as you can get and still live.

She moved in the other half of my house just before school started. Houses are cheap on my street because each house is half of a double house. Duplexes, they call them. So if you live in one half, you never know who or what is going to move into the other half, right on the other side of the wall. The houses are old and stand up tall and narrow, and the rooms inside each half are tall and narrow and dark and stacked on top of each other, so it's sort of like living in a filing cabinet. An old wooden filing cabinet with thin walls and holes. A guy down the street kept a boa constrictor as a pet, and it got into the wall somehow and through a little hole into Mr. Runkle's house next door, and he about died when he saw it warming its tummy on top of his television.

I like living where I do, though, because right down behind the row houses is country. Right at the end of our long, narrow backyard is pasture, then cornfield, then apple orchard. Towns are like that in Pennsylvania.

Anyway, it was a Saturday morning and I was in front of the TV set, watching Rocky and Bullwinkle, when Dad came in and said, "People moving in next door."

I went to the front window to look. There was the U-Haul and a man and woman and two teenage boys unloading it. A couple little girls were running around on the sidewalk, getting in the way. I figured out something about the same time I heard my dad tell my mother in a funny tone of voice, "Black family."

Mom said, "I don't care if they're purple, just so they're quiet."

My mom likes to say things like that and do the opposite of what people expect. Been that way since she was a kid. That's why she's an auto mechanic. Anyway, when she heard there were black people moving in next door, first thing she did was go over there to offer them coffee, and she dragged me with her. Next thing I know, I'm up in the front bedroom, saying hi to Shanterey, because I'm the same age as her.

So there was this tall girl with a sort of long, brown face and braids all over her head, and I'm telling her, "Hi, I'm Jenny Wetzel. From, you know, next door." And sort of waving my hand at the wall without any windows, the one between my place and hers.

Shanterey didn't smile or not smile. She just looked at me and nodded, and her hands stayed busy. Even though the beds were still coming in, she was unpacking a box and setting things on top of a dresser, the tallest of the three dressers crammed into the room.

I looked, and my mouth came open. She had

3

a little green felt pasture up there, with bottle-brush trees and a barn made out of a shoe box, and she was setting little horses in the barn and on the green cloth. Plastic model horses, mostly, but she had a few made out of china.

"Wow," I said, not because the model horses were anything different from mine, but because I didn't know black people liked horses. Black girls, anyway . . . at least this one . . . Shanterey . . . loved horses, the same way I did.

"They're neat," I said. "Can I see?"

She waited until her big brothers put a bunk bed in place, then climbed up on it so I could get to the dresser.

I didn't know which horse to pick up first. They were all pretty. My hand went for a bright chestnut one, a Stablemate I remembered from the Breyer folder. "Which one's this?" I asked, meaning which breed.

Shanterey said, "Wildfire."

That was what she'd named it, she meant. It was a good name for the chestnut horse with its color almost as red as fire. It made me think of cow ponies and wild horses, mustangs, and I didn't care anymore what breed the Stablemate was supposed to be. I set it down and picked up another, a gray one. "What's this one's name?" I wanted to know.

4

"Wildfire."

I looked up where she sat on the top bunk like a scrawny, black vulture, watching me. I said, "I thought you said the other one's name was Wildfire."

Shanterey said, "They're all named Wildfire."

I set the horse down and stared at her. She was finally smiling, sort of, but it wasn't the kind of smile I was used to. Not like she was teasing me. And before I could figure out if she was joking or what, my mom's voice came floating up the stairs. "Jennifer!"

I went down, and Shanterey swung off the bunk and came down the steep stairs behind me.

"We'd better go, Jen, and let these people get settled." That was just like a parent. First drag me over to visit. Then drag me away. "Are your children going to the public schools, Chela?"

That was Mrs. Lucas, Shanterey's mother. She nodded, moving her head up once slow, down once slow. "That's what we moved here for," she said. "We heard the schools were good here." She was tall, too, and she had the same quiet way about her as Shanterey.

"Good. Then Jenny and Shanterey will be in the same class," said Mom, talking a blue streak,

5

as usual. "Is it okay with you if Jenny walks with Shanterey? I don't like for her to walk to school alone. You hear so much about people trying to get kids into cars."

Chela Lucas didn't say anything, but she smiled as if she and my mother had a secret. Shanterey and I didn't look at each other.

I waited until we were around the corner of our own house, heading toward the kitchen door, before I said as sarcastic as I could, "Nice going, Mom."

"I thought so," she replied, and she started to hum to herself like a cat. I hate that.

It was one thing if I decided to be friends with Shanterey. It was another thing to have Mom pushing me into it. Even if Shanterey wasn't a black person, I would have felt like that.

Well, maybe.

By lunchtime I was still thinking about the new neighbors, and not because I was excited, either. I felt sort of mad because it should have been fun, having a girl my own age move in next door. I really did need someone to walk to school with and be friends with. All the people on my end of town were either real old or had brat kids a lot younger than me.

The Lucases were still moving stuff in. Sitting at our kitchen table, me and Mom and Dad

6

and my big sister, Stephanie, we could hear them wrestling it around. A yell sounded through the wall, and a crash as something fell over. Then we heard one of the little girls crying.

"How many kids did you say they had?" my dad asked my mom, meaning something different. She knew it as well as I did, but she pretended not to notice.

"Five," she said, not even looking up from her sandwich. "Two boys, three girls. The girls get the front bedroom, the boys get the middle, the parents get the back. Chela says it's amazing how many kids you can stack into a room if you have to."

Dad looked at her with a sour little smile, but all he said was, "With that many kids, you can forget about them not being noisy."

Mom said, "I think it's nice to hear people moving around over there again." But there was something tight in her voice.

Stephanie rolled her eyes. I just ate my Swiss cheese and kept quiet. I wished I could forget about the new neighbors, but the thumpings and bumpings and trompings on their side of the wall wouldn't let me. All my life old Mrs. Nace had lived over there, until she died, and she didn't make any more noise than your average mouse. Old Mrs. Nace hadn't been any fun, and

7

she hadn't had any kids for me to be friends with, but at least she hadn't made me feel . . . I didn't want to be prejudiced, but everything about the new neighbors made me feel uncomfortable. The way they fixed their hair, and the way their fingernails looked, different from mine, and everything. I mean, I watched "The Cosby Show" on TV, but it wasn't the same as being right in the house with black people. I didn't know where to look or how to act when I was around real black people.

And Shanterey. Huh. She was the strangest-looking of the bunch and a nut case for sure. A girl who named all her horses Wildfire.

Two

MONDAY morning, when the alarm went off, I swatted it, stretched, rolled over, and looked out my window, as always. The window was right at the head of the bed, and I had the back bedroom. I could see everything. It was like being in a lighthouse or something, because the wall dropped three tall stories to the back cellar door, and then the yard sloped away to hilly waves of trees and field and fence and trees again, with houses white like boats now and then. This morning it really looked like the sea, because it all grayed into distance and cloudy sky. It was going to rain, it was six A.M., and it was the first day of school.

9

Before eight I was on the sidewalk out in front of the Lucas place, waiting for Shanterey. My mom had given me orders before she went to work, and I knew by her tone that she meant what she said.

I still tried to find a way out. "Can't you just drive me?" I asked my dad as he headed out the door. He sells shoes, and he has to be in Harrisburg by nine-thirty.

"Heck, no," he said. "You do what your mother told you." And Stephanie was already gone, to catch the bus to the high school.

So there I was when Shanterey came out with her two little sisters, and all three of them were wearing dresses. Good dresses, too, like for going to church or something. The little girls looked cute, but Shanterey looked really dumb. White anklet socks on those black-slat legs of hers. I didn't know what to say to her.

So we walked off, and the little girls ran ahead, and Shanterey yelled after them to wait for us at the corner. Their names were Djuna and Chelsea, and they were in first and second grade. Little kids dress up for the first day of school a lot of the time, so they looked all right.

After a while I said to Shanterey, "We mostly wear pants to school." I was wearing black stretch pants and a fleece shirt of my sis-

ter's, big enough so it hung down to my knees.
I had borrowed it after she was out of the house.
I had borrowed a pair of her earrings, too, hoop
ones. I knew I looked cool. Maybe Shanterey
didn't have black stretch pants, but I figured any
old thing she had would look better than that
dress.

She looked at me and just nodded, once, and
said, "My mother made me."

I laughed out loud, because my mother was
making me walk with her. Then I felt funny
because maybe she would think I was laughing
at her, and I asked her, quick, "Do you like to
ride horses?"

She drew back her head as if to say, "Are you
kidding? Does a cat like fish? Does Superman
like to fly?" But what she said was, "Don't you?"

"Sure! I learned how at camp, one year."

Girl Scout camp. Walking and trotting
around and around a dusty ring, and the horses
hated all of us just for being alive; I could tell. I
had never got to canter. My horse wouldn't
canter, just trotted faster, till I felt like I was
sitting on top of a jackhammer. I didn't tell Shanterey that.

"Someday I want to learn how to jump," I
said.

We reached the first corner, and Shanterey

took each of her sisters by the hand before we crossed. Then she let them go again and said, "I only ever got to ride a few times. A friend of ours used to have a horse and let us kids ride it."

I said, teasing, "Was its name Wildfire?"

She gave me that same smile again, the one I couldn't understand, and said, "No. Its name was Pudge Wildfire."

Something about the way she said it made me laugh out loud again.

"Brown-and-white pinto," Shanterey added before I had to ask. "It was just a fat pony, really, not a horse."

"Was it slow?"

"Real slow. It had something wrong with its feet, and they got rid of it."

"Did you ever get to canter?" I asked.

She shook her head, and I started telling her again about how I was going to learn to jump. I talked about it pretty much all the way to school.

Water Street School was an old yellow-brick school, tall and skinny like our house or like Shanterey. In the morning all the kids gathered on the fenced-in blacktop, waiting for the opening bell. And everybody was always real early for the first day. As soon as we got close, I started looking for friends I hadn't seen since last year and waving at them and yelling hi. This was always the best part of the first day of school, and I always got, like, excited. So it took me a minute to notice that something was wrong. Nobody said anything, exactly, but either kids were too quiet or they were staring and whispering and giggling. At Shanterey. And at me, because I was walking with her.

Sheesh. All the staring eyeballs made my skin feel crawly, as if I was turning black, too.

"Hi, Jen!" Heather broke away from a group of eyeballs and came up to me. I always knew Heather was nice.

"Heather! Hi! C'mon, let's go find Becky." I started to run off. Mom had said I had to show Shanterey the way to the school, but she never said I had to show her the way to the room. I figured I was done baby-sitting her. But Heather didn't run after me.

"Who's your friend?" she said. The way she said "friend" made it sound slimy, somehow. And Shanterey was standing right there, if Heather wanted to talk to her. Me, I just wanted to get away from her, before I caught something. Like blackness cooties.

"That's Shanterey," I said. "She just moved in. C'mon!"

Heather turned and looked Shanterey in the face, though she had to tilt her head back to do it. "That's a funny name," she said. Then she came with me.

"Black people have funny names," she said to me. I didn't say anything.

We found Becky and Lori and Katie and a whole bunch of other kids, and we talked and giggled a lot and clowned around and settled who was going to sit with who, and everybody liked my earrings. But I kept on noticing Shanterey standing by the school wall with her little sisters. Who could help noticing her, in that dress and everything? Kids kept walking past her, real quiet, and taking looks. The little girls were hanging onto Shanterey's hands like they were lost.

When the bell rang, I yelled at Heather, "Save me a seat!" and I found myself going to Shanterey to show her and her sisters the way to their rooms after all.

So I ended up coming into the room with Shanterey, and a little late, too, because of her kid sisters, and everybody had a good look. And Heather didn't save me a seat, either. I ended up sitting next to a boy. I could have spit. And old Mr. Hoffman, the teacher, didn't even blink when he saw Shanterey and showed her where to sit, but the first thing he did when he saw me was make me take off my earrings and give them

14

to him till the end of the day, because he said they weren't safe. They might catch on something, he said. Sheesh.

Then, to top it all off, it started to rain, not just a thunderstorm but a real rain, so I knew we wouldn't be able to go outside for recess. That wasn't fair. It wasn't supposed to rain the first day of school.

By the time lunch finally came, I was starved, and sleepy, because I wasn't used to getting up so early over the summer, and kind of grouchy. I was glad I had packed a lunch, because Shanterey was buying, and kids who packed sat separate from kids who bought. So at least I didn't have to make myself sit with her. Which I kind of felt I ought to.

The thing was, nobody sat with her. Which I noticed, because I was staring at her all the time, just like everybody else.

Some of the kids went to the gym after lunch. But Heather and Becky and a lot of us girls went back to the room. Becky put a record on the record player, and some of us started to dance. After a while Shanterey came in.

I was dancing, and dancing made me feel good. I felt ready to be her friend again. "Hey, Shanterey!" I yelled. "Come on and dance!"

"Yeah, Shanterey!" yelled Heather. "Dance!"

15

But she didn't say it the same way I had.

Shanterey's face didn't change, but her voice came out hard and flat, and she said, "Black people got rhythm, right? Well, not this one. You dance." And she sat down at her desk.

"Aw, c'mon!" said Heather, nasty-nice. "Do the moonwalk for us, like Michael Jackson!"

Shanterey sat scrunched-down in her seat, and I felt like I wanted to go somewhere else. So I went to the girls' room, by myself, and I don't know what they said to her after that.

It was a long day. At the end of it, when I got my earrings back from Mr. Hoffman, it was still raining hard, and I hadn't brought an umbrella because umbrellas aren't cool, and I knew my parents were both at work, and so were Shanterey's. I was going to have to walk home in the rain. With Shanterey.

She was waiting for me in the hallway with little Djuna and Chelsea, and we all went out the playground door, where kids were supposed to go. We didn't go out into the rain quite yet, because of the crowd. A lot of kids were standing huddled under the roof near the doors, waiting for their rides. Even though we were all packed in so tight we could barely move, some kids squealed and made a point of pushing back from the black kids. Not everybody. But some.

I started to think maybe I could catch a ride with a friend. I was not allowed to walk home alone, but Shanterey and her sisters could walk home by themselves okay. I tried to look around over people's heads to see who I knew, and just then somebody, I don't know who, gave me a hard push and hissed in my ear, "Nigger lover!"

I went out in the rain, and Shanterey came with me, and we walked away. Shanterey and I didn't say much the whole way home. The rain was running down our necks, and anyway, it hadn't been a very good day.

Three

I DECIDED I was going to have to side with the others against Shanterey if I was going to keep my friends. I had to walk to school and home with her. I couldn't do anything about that, but I didn't have to be nice to her in school. Nobody had said I did. And school was a whole different world from the neighborhood and home. It was kids' turf.

"How was school today?" my dad asked me Tuesday night at supper.

"Okay."

"Anything new?"

"Nuh-uh."

"What did you learn?"

"Nothing much."

In fact, I had learned to leave a tack on Shanterey's chair and make sure everybody noticed and knew who did it except her. She didn't sit on it when she came back from the blackboard. She just picked it off and didn't say anything to Mr. Hoffman. I got the idea she was used to looking for tacks on her chair. But that wasn't the point. The point was, the kids knew I was against her, too.

And I had learned to laugh with the others when somebody wrote "Nigger Elementary" in chalk on the front sidewalk.

That's pretty much how it went all that week. Mr. Hoffman was a good teacher, so nobody picked on Shanterey in class. Except, I guess, me, with my tack. But during lunch and recess he wasn't around, and sometimes the boys chanted dirty stuff at her. And us girls would go off and giggle with each other and plan what we were going to do to her. We had already done some graffiti in the girls' room—I was the lookout, and it was exciting and kind of fun. But even though they were being friends with me, I didn't feel good about my friends, the way I had the year before. They didn't seem as nice to me. Especially Heather. Sometimes I didn't like Heather much at all. But everybody else liked her, so I wanted her to like me.

Heather wanted me to get the Lucases' unlisted number so we could have a slumber party and make anonymous phone calls to their house all night. Mom had it on a paper by the phone, so that was easy. I didn't even have to talk to Shanterey to get it. I guess she knew the score. We weren't talking much on our way to and from school, not even about horses.

Which is what happened next. A horse happened, I mean.

On Saturday morning, when I woke up and stretched and rolled over and looked out my window, there was a palomino horse shining like gold fire in the pasture right behind the house, and my mouth came open so far I squeaked.

It was early yet—I had got used to waking up early for school—and the horse was standing with its head up, looking around, and there was September mist in the air, and the sun was hitting off the horse and the mist so that it looked as if the horse was standing in a halo. In a minute the horse put its head down and started to graze, and then it didn't look as special anymore. But still, my first thought was, Shanterey's got to see this. It was a weekend, and we weren't at school. I could be nice to her if I wanted.

But then a thought hit me, how I could play a little trick on her and tell the kids about it on Monday.

So I got dressed, fast, and went over to Shanterey's house without having breakfast or even watching TV. I was there half to show her the horse and half to fool her.

I saw her at the kitchen table. She was just a black shape in the dim light, but it wasn't hard to tell it was her. Nobody else had bony shoulders like her, with her head riding on top of them like a hood ornament. I yelled in the screen door, "Shanterey! C'mon out! I got to show you something!"

There was a murmur as her mother told her it was okay for her to go, and then she came out, not letting the screen door slam. She wasn't smiling, and I guess she knew maybe I was up to something, but I didn't care. Right away I led her off at a trot across the street, away from the back of the house and the horse. I was betting she hadn't seen the horse yet, because she had the front bedroom, and the big old lilac bush behind her house hid the view from the kitchen window.

And I figured she didn't know her way around town yet, because she had to sit her little sisters after school till her folks got home. And I knew they didn't come outside much. There was unpacking to do, maybe. Or maybe they just liked to stay in after a long day at school, watch TV. Sure, that had to be why they stayed in all the time.

So I was hoping I could confuse Shanterey pretty good if I moved fast.

I took her down a shortcut between two garages to a back alley through an empty cigar factory and out the hole in the fence to a woodlot and down the junkyard hill to a dirt road and then we struck off cross-country. We were clear out of sight of town, but I knew it was just on the other side of a little hill and some trees. And we were circling around it, but country roads are so twisty it would be hard for Shanterey to know that. She would think we were miles away from home before we were done.

"How much farther?" she asked after a while. She didn't look nervous, and she wasn't panting or anything, because she had long legs. I was puffing from trying to hurry her.

"You'll see," I puffed.

"What's this thing you want to show me?"

"You'll see."

We hit a hard road and followed it to a farm lane. Then I led her up the lane, past the farmhouse, and back through the orchard to the pasture. It was the middle of the morning by then, and I was half-afraid the horse would be gone for some reason. But there he stood, and he was a real palomino, with a thick, creamy mane and tail.

"All *right!*" Shanterey breathed, and that long face of hers lit up with the first real grin I'd seen on it.

"He's so pretty," I said. He really was, and not just the color. Now that we were closer, I could see that his head was small, with big eyes and a wide forehead. "I think he's an Arabian."

She shook her head but never looked away from the horse. "They don't have palomino Arabians."

"They don't?" I never knew that.

"And he's heavy for an Arab. He could be part Arab, though."

We climbed the fence without even talking about it and walked into the pasture to go see the horse. He was grazing on a little hill, and as we walked upslope, I said to Shanterey, "You can see him anytime you want to. There's your house, right over there." And I pointed toward the town coming into view over the rise. Our backyards, hers and mine, ran right down to the pasture fence opposite the one we had come in.

She looked at me, still grinning. "You turkey," she said, and I knew she understood the trick I had played on her, but she didn't mind because she was so excited about the horse. And I didn't mind that she didn't mind.

The horse threw his head up and snorted as

we walked up to him. We put our hands out and coaxed, and he stood still and let us come up to him and pat him. His hair lay silky-smooth, but his mane was like a rough, white, windblown cloud. He had white on all four feet and a white star on his forehead.

"How's this for a Wildfire?" I asked Shanterey.

"Right on," she said.

We patted the horse until he got tired of it and put his head down to graze, and then we stood beside him with our hands on his mane. After a while I saw a man coming up the pasture from the house. Shanterey saw him, too, and stopped smiling.

"It's all right," I told her, proud to be able to tell her that. "It's just old man Seitz. I've known him since I was born, practically."

He was real Dutchified, and he always called me Chenny. My sister called me that sometimes, too, because she knew I hated it.

"Hey, Mr. Seitz!" I yelled as he got closer. "Where'd you get the neat horse?"

He came up to us, and he said to me, "Chenny, you sprout," just the way he always did, but he was scowling hard. I couldn't figure out what was wrong.

"Some people like lawn ornaments," he said

to me. "I always wanted a pretty horse in the pasture, is all."

"He's *real* pretty," I said to make Mr. Seitz stop scowling. "Is he Arabian?"

"Part. Part quarter horse." Mr. Seitz just looked at me, never at Shanterey, but I sort of felt her standing next to me in his head.

I said, "Mr. Seitz, this is Shanterey. She's my new neighbor."

He nodded, but not at Shanterey, and he took a deep breath, like he was working himself up to something. Then he said all at once, "Chenny, you're welcome to come see this horse anytime. You ride him, too. But I don't want no nigger on my land or messing with my horse." Then for the first time he looked straight at Shanterey, and his eyes went narrow and mean.

Shanterey jerked her hand back from the horse as if Wildfire's golden neck had just gone red-hot, and she took a quick step back.

"Chungle bunnies ain't welcome here," Mr. Seitz said.

Shanterey started away without waiting for me, but I ran after her and said, "Let's get out of here," like it was my idea.

"Now, you, Chenny, you're welcome anytime," Mr. Seitz called after me in a high voice.

I didn't answer. Shanterey and I didn't say

25

anything to each other, either. We went through the far pasture fence, and she went running up through her yard on those long legs of hers, and I went panting up behind her. Mrs. Lucas came out on the porch to shake a rug just as Shanterey tore up the steps.

"Shanterey!" her mother called. "Did you see there's a horse down behind us?"

Shanterey pushed past her without answering and slammed into the house. Mrs. Lucas stood there staring at the screen door, and I hurried around the corner of their house and over to my own place so I wouldn't have to talk to her.

Four

THE next day, Sunday, I went down to ride the horse. I felt funny about Mr. Seitz, as if I didn't want to see him again real soon, but I figured there was no reason for me not to ride his horse. It wasn't like I got to ride every day. Anyway, Mr. Seitz and his wife would be in church. That's why I waited until Sunday morning.

I checked to see if their car was gone, just to make sure. It was. Then I went into the big, empty barn and found a cardboard box of horse stuff, an old halter and a couple ropes and a few beat-up brushes, like that. No saddle or bridle. The flap of the box had "Cody's things" printed on it in marker. So that was the horse's real name. Cody.

I took the halter and snapped the ropes onto it like reins and went out to where the palomino was grazing. Wow, he was pretty. And he let me come up to him and pat him and put the halter on his head. Then he let me lead him over to the fence. He wouldn't stand very still beside the fence, but I finally got onto him by letting him graze while I climbed the fence and reached my leg over his bare back. Then I pulled his head up and kicked him a little to make him walk. And he walked around and let me ride him.

And the sun was shining, and the pasture was full of white and yellow and purple flowers so tall I could pick them as we rode by, and a blue butterfly flew up and hung in the air around Wildfire's ears—Wildfire, I still thought of the horse as Wildfire; it was a lot better name than Cody. The butterfly followed along with us wherever we went. It seemed to love Wildfire. I couldn't control the horse much to make him go where I wanted, but I didn't care. We were in the pasture, so it didn't matter. I liked him to take me where he wanted to. It was wonderful, riding Wildfire.

And it was hollow, somehow, and it hurt. But I didn't want to think about why.

I decided I was going to canter, and I kicked the horse to make him go faster. He jerked into a trot that almost bumped me off. I kicked him some more, bouncing around on his back, but he just threw up his head and swished his tail and trotted till my teeth rattled. I finally gave up and pulled on my rope reins, and then he didn't want to slow down.

I got off when I finally got him stopped. Seitzes would be coming home from church soon, anyway, and I didn't want to talk to them. I put the halter and stuff back in the barn, and I went home.

At lunch, when my mother asked me where I'd been all morning, I said, "Just walking around." I hadn't told her or my father anything about Shanterey and Wildfire and Mr. Seitz, or about school, or anything. It all seemed too dirty, somehow, to talk about.

Out of nowhere, as if she was thinking some of the same things I was thinking, my sister, Stephanie, said, "Dwayne and Quinn Lucas been getting beat up after school every day this week."

Shanterey's two older brothers, she meant. They went to the high school with Steph. Both my parents stopped nodding over their tomato soup and jerked their heads up, looking at Stephanie.

"When you say 'beat up,'" my mother said, "I hope you don't mean really beat up."

"Well, hassled," Steph admitted. "They got

hit on once, though. Quinn had a bloody nose one day on the bus. They fight pretty good," she added.

My mom was frowning, and my father said, "There's no reason for that. Lucases are decent people. Nice as anybody."

We all sat a minute and listened to the sounds from next door. Lucases had turned out not to be noisy during the week after all. But this Sunday they were having their friends and family up from Harrisburg to see their new place, so we heard plenty of chatter and laughing going on in their half of the house. It was good to listen to.

Mom looked at me. "How are Shanterey and Djuna and Chelsea getting along, Jen?"

"Okay, I guess," I said, and I took a big bite of my grilled-cheese sandwich so I wouldn't have to talk.

"Little kids aren't as mean to new kids," said Steph.

I excused myself as soon as I could and went outside.

I really did walk around that afternoon, all over town, and didn't head home until close to suppertime.

Old Mrs. Raffensberger was sitting out on her front porch a few doors from mine when I went by, and I stopped to say hi. She was always out on her porch, even in winter sometimes, and I always stopped to say hi. I don't know why, except that I'd been doing it all my life. Mom must have told me sometime I had to be polite to Mrs. Raffensberger. It was a pain, because she hardly ever had anything nice to say.

"I saw you out cavorting on that horse," she said this time. "You just watch yourself, missy. You don't know what that horse is going to do."

Of course she saw. She always saw everything. She saw me pick up a feather once and yelled that I was going to get lice. She saw me pat a dog and barked, "You don't know where that dog's nose has been!" For a minute I thought of the blue butterfly lighting on Wildfire's white mane and wondered if Mrs. Raffensberger could find something bad to say about that. Probably. She probably knew of some disease spread by blue butterflies or something bad that would happen if you saw one.

Some people came out of the Lucases' house, and Mrs. Raffensberger clawed a pair of binoculars out from under her skirt where it lay on the glider beside her.

"The way I figure it," she pronounced, bringing the binoculars up to her eyes, "them Negroes next to you is drug dealers." She had a pad of paper and a pencil in her lap, and she scrawled down a number with her shaky old hand as Mrs. Lucas's parents drove away. "These here license numbers are for the police."

What was the matter with everybody? Was the whole world going crazy, or was I? "Why the heck would you think something like that?" I burst out.

She put down the binoculars and looked at me like I just grew an extra head. "How else would they pay for the house?"

I stared at her. She had buzzard eyes, and veins showing like purple worms on the end of her nose. Good grief, how did anybody pay for a house?

After a minute she sort of rapped out, "Well, I must admit, the children are clean enough. I haven't seen a speck of dirt on any of those children."

Shanterey had been able to get away with not wearing a dress to school after the first day, but she wore clothes that looked too new and pressed. All of them did. The boys wore tube socks so white they about hurt your eyes. The little girls wore matched outfits without a spot or a hole on them anywhere. I glanced down at my own old jeans. Plenty of dirt on me, since I'd been horseback riding. Yet Mrs. Raffensberger didn't seem to mind talking to me.

It wasn't fair. It just wasn't fair, any of it.

I went home and did my schoolwork and went to bed early, without watching "Disney" or anything. The next day Shanterey and I walked to school without saying much, and especially without saying anything about Wildfire.

When we got to school, I didn't go off with Heather and Becky and that gang. I didn't feel like telling them about the trick I had played on Shanterey anymore. I just stood against the wall, next to Shanterey. People whispered and giggled and yelled stuff at both of us, but I sort of didn't notice them. I felt like I was floating somewhere between two places, not quite in one and not really in the other, either.

At lunchtime I sat next to Shanterey to eat, and I still didn't say much of anything to her. At recess we just walked around together, side by side. We didn't say anything or do anything. We didn't pay any attention to the kids trying to make us mad.

By the end of the day half the kids in our class were going crazy because they couldn't figure me out. I knew how they felt. I couldn't figure me out, either.

Shanterey, though, was cool. She just waited to see what was going on.

It got plain to both of us when we walked out the playground door to go home. It was like walking into a trap. I had a choice about how to act, and I stopped floating and chose.

Just about all the kids in the fifth grade were waiting for us. Most of them were just standing around like they were going to watch a show, but there was this boy, and some girl had put mascara or something black all over his face and put a pair of big, ugly red lips on him with lipstick. He danced up in front of Shanterey, jerked his head over to one side, and rolled his eyes and stuck out his tongue like he was dead. Some of the other kids started chanting, "K-K-K! K-K-K! K—"

Shanterey's face hardly moved at all, but I went a little crazy.

"What's the matter with you kids!" I screamed, and when I start yelling, my dad always said, I can stop a truck. Everybody heard me, and I mostly drowned out the chanting. "You're nothing but a bunch of—" I couldn't remember the word, and that made me even madder. "You're prejudiced! You're worse'n dog breath! You oughta all be ashamed! You judge a person by their color, you don't even give them a chance! Shanterey's nice, you get to know her once!" Even though I didn't know her all that well myself. "Real nice! And you're sure as heck not! You're a bunch of snot-nose, half-baked *bigots!*" I got that right, finally.

34

My throat hurt from yelling so loud, but the rest of me felt better.

Of course it didn't do any good. I knew it wouldn't. Some of the ones who were just watching walked away, but the ones who were yelling got worse. Shanterey and I walked through them to where her little sisters were waiting for us on the playground, and we headed home, and I was puffing as if I had run a race, hot all over. And some kids yelled stuff at us and jostled us the whole time, and some of them followed us, still yelling.

"Buncha niggers!"

"Nigger lover!"

"Jenny, Jenny, four-by-four, couldn't find the bathroom door. . . ."

After about a block they quit, though, and the voices faded away behind us. I puffed my lips and blew my breath out like a tired horse, and Shanterey turned and looked at me and finally said something. She had on that funny smile of hers.

"Good going, Wetzel," she said. "But couldn't you just say I was a cool dude? Now I got to be 'real nice.' Sheesh."

Five

IT didn't happen right away, that I got to be best friends with Shanterey. I think she liked me okay, but she didn't really trust me for a while, not after the way I'd been just as bad as the others that first week. And it took me a while, too, to get used to going against my friends and liking a black person.

It took us a while to really talk to each other, even. We started, that first day walking home after I called everybody bigots, but there was a lot of stuff we didn't say.

"I didn't mean anything bad, asking you to dance that time," I told Shanterey. "I just thought you might like to."

She nodded. I really hadn't meant anything that time. She knew there were a lot of other times, but she didn't say that. She said, "I look like a freak when I dance."

And I noticed how she bent her head over when she walked, and remembered how she scrooched down in her chair in class a lot of the time, and I understood one thing, anyway. Shanterey thought she was too tall. I didn't know what was safe to say about dancing, so I didn't say any more.

I said, "And I never thought Mr. Seitz was going to act that way. Really. I've known him since I can remember, and I never knew him to be mean before."

"Then you never knew him with a black person before," said Shanterey, not asking, just saying it, with a kind of gloomy fun in her voice.

"Right," I admitted.

And I had been mean myself that day, taking her the long way to see the horse. I had been seeing a new, ugly side to a lot of people, including me, and I didn't like it.

But still, I didn't tell Shanterey about giving her phone number to Heather, or what the girls planned to do with it, or anything. And I didn't tell her about how I went to ride Wildfire.

And I kept going to ride Wildfire, too, a few

more times. I tried every way I could think of to enjoy that horse even though I knew Shanterey couldn't. I spent one whole Saturday afternoon just braiding his white mane with fall flowers and making a fall-flower crown for myself and riding out in the pasture that way. I set up a little jump made of old lumber from the barn and tried to make Wildfire go over it. Since I still couldn't even get him to canter or go where I wanted, that was hopeless. But I tried. And a couple of times I fell off. And I spent a lot of time just riding around the pasture, feeling sort of lonely.

School was awful. I didn't have any friends but Shanterey. Most of the kids stayed away from me like I had some sort of disease, and some of them picked on me the same way they picked on her. Except they didn't call me nigger. They called me Pretzel Wetzel, which was so silly it stunk. I'm not built anything like a pretzel. More like a thick stick.

"Hey, nigger lover!"

"Pretzel!"

"Hey, how's your black girlfriend, you faggot?"

Every day and every day. Sometimes I wanted to play sick and stay home from school, but then Shanterey would have had to face it alone. Anyway, my mom was pretty sharp about things like that. She knew sick from "sick." So I went. All the hassling hurt so bad sometimes I wanted to scream or cry. Sometimes I chased after kids or shouted stuff back, but Shanterey never did.

"How can you just walk along like you don't hear them?" I asked her after school one day. We were up in her room, playing with her model horses. We played with all the little plastic Wildfires almost every day after school, giving them boyfriends and stuff. Ebony Wildfire went with Ivory Wildfire, and Wildfire Sun Chief, the chestnut quarter horse, went with Wildfire Moonlight, the gray. Sometimes we went over to my place with them to get away from her sisters. Getting together after school and on weekends seemed to almost make up for school sometimes. I didn't feel funny about Shanterey anymore. I liked everything about her: her big feet, all the dark, rich colors in her skin, the downy hair on the sides of her narrow face, the way she stretched out and got taller when she finally started to relax, everything.

We didn't usually talk about school when we got together, but this time I did.

"How can you just ignore them?"

Shanterey shrugged those big, skinny shoulders of hers. "Yelling back doesn't do any good."

I knew that. I saw how it just sort of encouraged them. But I got so mad. . . . "But how can you *help* it?" I asked Shan. I called her Shan sometimes.

"You get used to it," she said, and she wrinkled her nose in a certain way, and I stared at her.

"Don't tell me they picked on you where you went to school before!" I knew the Lucases had moved out to our town from Harrisburg, to get away from the city schools. I had figured Shanterey had been in a mostly black school before.

She shrugged and turned back to the model horses. Whatever had happened to her before, she wasn't going to tell me about it. She said, "Let's go down and get something to eat."

I didn't feel funny about the rest of the Lucases anymore, either. Djuna and Chelsea were just regular brat sisters, so cute you wanted to kill them half the time and hug them the rest. Dwayne and Quinn were just regular big brothers, a pain in the butt. Mrs. Lucas was nice. Not nice like the people I used to think were nice, like Heather. Really nice. Mr. Lucas worked for the army somewhere in Harrisburg, but he didn't act like it. He never seemed to yell at all.

I was still at Shanterey's house, sitting at the

40

kitchen table, eating corn curls, when Mrs. Lucas came in from work. She worked at the fancy clothing store in the mall, and she had to dress nice, and she always looked beautiful when she came home. She was tall, too, and I knew someday Shanterey would look like her and be gorgeous. But Mrs. Lucas always went upstairs and changed into jeans as soon as she could.

This evening she had just said hi when the phone rang on the wall beside her head. She got a tight look on her face before she answered it. I glanced at Shan and saw the same look on her.

It was for Shanterey, but instead of handing it over, Mrs. Lucas gave her daughter a questioning glance and said into the receiver, "Who is it, please?"

Then she made a face and just hung up without saying any more.

"Was it them again?" Shanterey asked. I started to get a sick feeling in the pit of my stomach, because I figured I knew who "them" was.

Mrs. Lucas nodded.

"What'd they say this time?"

"Just the usual filth. Kids. They don't know any words I don't know." Mrs. Lucas sat down at the table with us and gave her daughter a tired smile. "I'd just laugh if it wasn't that they call so late at night. I swear, I don't know what sort of parents would let their children stay up that late, let alone use the phone.''

My mouth felt dry when I said, "Can't the phone company do anything?"

"They could trace the calls and press charges. But don't you think that would just make more trouble, Jenny?"

Shanterey's mother was looking at me as if she really wanted my opinion. "I guess," I said. "Maybe you should just change your phone number."

"We could do that. But I'll tell you what really upsets me." Mrs. Lucas got up and started to walk around the room for no reason. "We gave that number only to people we thought we could trust. Now we get these calls, and I keep wondering who we were wrong about."

I swallowed hard and said, "It was me." I didn't believe what I was saying. Any kid with any sense would have kept quiet. But I had to try to make it right for them somehow.

Mrs. Lucas swung around and stared at me, and Shanterey stared, too, and said to me, "What do you mean, it was you? You're sitting here! You didn't make that call."

"I mean it was my fault." I was talking to the tablecloth, but then I made myself look at Shanterey when I said, "It was back at the beginning of school, when I still wanted Heather and them to like me. I gave them the number."

And I had been worrying about it ever since. Knew I should have gone to an adult and told. Knew I'd get killed by adults and kids both if I did. Now who was I telling? Mrs. Lucas! The one getting the dirty phone calls, getting waked up at night. She had a right to do worse than kill me.

I made myself look at her, and a big, soft smile spread across her face, and she said, "It's all right." She came over to me and mussed my hair. It was the first time she'd ever touched me. "Really, it's all right now," she said. "We can just get the number changed, and that will be the end of it." She patted me, then went upstairs to change her clothes.

But Shanterey was leaning way back in her chair and staring at me. I looked at her, then mumbled, "I guess I'd better go home," and I went.

Then next day, walking to school, she was real quiet with me, and I knew I'd put myself in a fix. If Shanterey turned against me, I wouldn't have any friends left at all. I wasn't sure my old friends would take me back, and I wasn't sure I wanted them to. Shanterey was the one I wanted for a friend.

43

On the way home I sort of took the bit in my teeth and said, "You mad?"

"Not really." She wasn't looking at me, but she must have felt me looking at her, and she said, "Well, I was still mad this morning. But now I'm mostly just thinking."

"About what?"

She said, "Back that first week, somebody put a tack on my chair, right in class. Was that you?"

Something in her voice dared me to tell her the truth, and I said, "Uh-huh."

We were quiet for a little bit, and then she said, "Okay. Tell me something else."

"What?"

"Who drew that picture of me on the chalkboard?"

I knew the one she meant. They had put a big, hairy, you know, thing on her, then put her name underneath to be sure everybody understood. And I knew who had done it, too. A couple of the boys, Neil and Kevin.

But I said, "I ain't telling."

Then she knew it wasn't me, and she turned on me with a wicked grin and crooned, "Chenny! Chen-ny! Nyaah!" And she tapped me with her long hand and ran.

"Hey!" I yelled. "No fair!" And I chased her.

44

And if it hadn't been for her having to stop to cross her sisters at the next corner, I never would have caught her. She could outrun me anytime. And she was laughing out loud.

And somehow after all that we knew we were really friends for keeps.

Six

So that was when I stopped riding Wildfire.

It was getting cold and wet, anyway. The leaves were all down, the sky was gray, the ground was brown, the wind blew all the time. But that wasn't why I quit. I wouldn't have minded going down in the cold and grooming Wildfire's winter coat, thick like velvet. But I didn't. I knew there would be snow, and I knew I wanted to get up on Wildfire and ride him in the snow. I could imagine what it would be like. The white flakes would lie on his white mane, and his hooves would bite through the snow, and his nostrils would flare, and his breath would come out in dragon-puffs.

And I knew I wouldn't do it, because Shanterey couldn't.

I said to her, "I've been riding Mr. Seitz's horse every once in a while."

She just nodded. She knew before I told her.

I said, "I'm not going down there anymore unless you can, too."

"Okay," she said.

And it was okay. But that didn't mean I wanted to look at that horse every morning out of my bedroom window, once I had made up my mind not to ride him. When I'd first wake up, I'd look out the window before I remembered not to, and Wildfire was always somewhere in sight, shining like a horse made of gold, and he was always so beautiful it hurt.

My sister, Stephanie, had the front bedroom. When we were both upstairs at night, when our parents weren't listening, I started asking her to trade with me.

"How come?" She would be busy with her books or her rock-star magazines or her personal beauty or something, and she didn't like me coming into her room much.

"I just want to." I wasn't about to tell her how come. It wasn't like it was some big deal. I mean, we didn't have to move the beds or the furniture or anything, just our stuff.

47

"You're going to have to do better than that, Brat, if you expect me to move." She always called me Brat except when she was mad. Then she called me Snotty Brat.

"Aw, c'mon, Steph! Pleeeease—"

"No! Get out of here!"

But I kept after her, every night for about a week, and she finally said okay, if I did all the work *for* her. I said I would make her bed and everything, and I did. I spent most of Thanksgiving vacation moving my stuff to her room and her stuff to mine.

When I got everything arranged in my new room—my own toy horses and model horses and horse figurines and horse books on the shelves, my stuffed monkey on the dresser with all my junk jewelry on him, and my new Michael J. Fox poster up over my bed—everything looked so good that I invited Shanterey over to see. She already knew my horses, of course. They were all named Wildfire now, too. But she was used to seeing my room in the back of the house, and in a mess.

"All *right,*" she approved. "But what you got that honky on the wall for?"

"That's Michael J. Fox, Shan!"

"He's a *honky,* Wetzel!" She grinned at me, and I knew she was teasing. "Why don't you put up a cool black dude?"

"Like Michael Jackson?"

"Sure." She tried out my new bed, stretching out on the quilt. "Hey," she said. "Your bed's right next to mine now."

It was true. My bed was along the wall between the two houses, and so was hers. When she went home and went to sleep, we would be probably no more than a few inches apart. We could talk to each other if it wasn't for the wall between her place and mine, the wall without windows.

"Michael and Michael are back to back," Shanterey said.

I knew what she meant. She had a Michael Jackson poster on the wall above her bed. It was on the other side of the wall from my Michael J. Fox poster, except it was sort of squeezed in underneath the top bunk. I knew it couldn't be all that great for Shan, having to share a room with her two sisters. But she didn't complain, and she seemed glad for me that I had the big front room all to myself.

When I was getting ready for bed that night I thought I heard somebody moving around in Shanterey's room, and after I turned off the light and crawled in, I tried tapping on the wall. And after a minute Shanterey tapped back.

This was going to be great, having my room next to Shanterey's; I knew it already. Though I

49

didn't know yet how good and how much trouble it was going to be.

And Mr. Seitz and his horse were to thank for it all.

He must have heard me thinking about him, because the next day, the last day of Thanksgiving vacation, he came to the house. I heard a knock on the kitchen door, and I opened it up without thinking to look first, and there he was.

And there was Shanterey, sitting at the kitchen table right in front of him, because we had been playing Parcheesi. But he didn't nod at her or anything. His eyes slid right over her as if she wasn't there.

"Chenny," he said to me. "How you been?"

"Fine."

"Me and the missus want to go away once. She wants to know, would you take care of the horse for us." He wasn't really asking, just sort of telling. Neighbors expected these things of neighbors. "Feed, water, like that."

A few months before I would have said, "Yes, sure, I would love to do it." And a few weeks before I would have at least thought about it, because I really would love taking care of Wildfire, almost as if he was my own horse. . . . But by then I knew the right answer, and I think I would have said the same even if Shan wasn't sitting there.

"If Shanterey can come, too," I said.

"Who's that?"

Shanterey said quietly, "Me."

And he still didn't look at her. But his face changed so I felt like I didn't know him, and he said to me, "I told you before, I don't want no coon on my land or messing with my horse."

"Then I can't come feed," I told him. "Sorry." I really did mean sorry, too. It would have been fun. Better than fun. Wonderful.

And I was sorry, too, because I felt good and scared. I felt like he was going to come through the door at me.

He didn't, but his face went stony white, he was so mad, and his lips pulled back, and he couldn't seem to get his breath to talk. He was so mad he couldn't even yell at me. After a minute he turned to go, and the way he walked back to his car was like a crazy person, huffing and stomping and whipping his arms around. After I closed the door, I heard his engine roar and his tires squeal as he pulled out onto the street.

I stood there shaking, and Shanterey came and stood beside me. She didn't say I should go take care of the horse, either, and I'm glad she didn't. It would have been garbage if she had. She knew what friends were for. She just said, "Jeez," sort of soft, and her face looked like she saw trouble coming.

I put my hand on her arm, I felt so shaky, and she hugged me.

We talked a little, and it took us a while to get back to the Parcheesi game. I had just rolled the dice for my turn, and it was doubles, when the phone rang.

"Lord," I said, because I had been getting some hate calls, too, from some of the kids at school; I could guess which ones. But this call was from Mom, and she never called from work unless something was wrong.

"Jenny! Mr. Seitz came by here, and he's *livid*. Says he asked you to take care of his horse, and you sassed him. What in the world—"

"I never sassed him!"

She wasn't saying I did. I guess she knew I wasn't likely to talk back to a person with a horse to ride. I shouldn't have yelled like that. Her voice sounded edgy when she said, "Then *what* is going on?"

I didn't want to talk about it in front of Shan. "Can I tell you later, Mom?"

"No! Right now! He's still here."

I mumbled, "He, like, calls Shan names and stuff, and he won't let her come down to his place." I sort of heard Mom listening over the clanging noises of the garage, and my voice got stronger. "What I told him was, I'd take care of Wildfire, his horse I mean, if Shan could come too."

Mom didn't say a thing for a minute. All I heard was wrenches banging and air hoses dinging, and I said, "Mom?"

"I'm here." All the edge had gone out of her voice. It sounded real quiet, like she was thinking hard. "Tell me exactly what Mr. Seitz said."

"Mom! I can't tell you that! Shan's right here."

"I'm going," Shan said, and she unfolded herself from her chair and headed out the door.

So I told Mom the names Mr. Seitz had called Shanterey, and when I was done she said in the same soft voice, "I'll take care of it." She told me to stay in the house, and she hung up.

A little while later the phone rang again, and it was Shanterey. "You all right?"

"Sure. Why wouldn't I be all right?"

"Your mom called my mom at the shop." That was something that had never happened before. "Said Mr. Seitz was making threats. Said it was probably just hot air, but she wanted us to know. My brothers are home, but I'm still supposed to stay in the house. You want to come over here?"

"My mom told me to stay here."

Shan sort of laughed. "Sheesh, it's practically the same house!"

"You'd hear me if I screamed," I said, and I told her bye and hung up.

I wasn't really scared. Just the same, I jumped when the door opened and my mom came in.

"You quit early!"

"They sent me home. Mr. Seitz got so loud, my boss couldn't help noticing something was wrong." She looked at me, then came over and touched my hair, and said, "I think Mr. Seitz wanted me to horsewhip you or something. Honey, I wish you would have told me what was going on."

I hate to admit it, but I grabbed her around the waist and started to bawl.

That was a long evening. After supper Mom and Dad wanted me to tell about Mr. Seitz all over again. It was not that they didn't believe me. They just wanted to get all the facts straight. Stephanie listened in, and for a wonder she didn't have anything snotty to say. And after I was done, I got up the nerve to ask, "Was it all right, what I did?" By adults' rules, I meant. I knew it was right by kids' rules. But was it going to cause my family trouble? Were they going to be mad at me?

Mom said, "It's a judgment call, Hon. I think you did the right thing."

Dad said, "I probably would have just gone ahead and fed the stupid horse." He sounded sort of depressed, but I could tell he wasn't mad at me, any more than Mom was. And Mom looked at him with her eyebrows raised.

"You going to offer Seitz to feed it?"

"Heck, no. Not after today." He got up and stretched and sort of grinned at me. "I just hate trouble with the neighbors, is all."

Stephanie said, loud, "Well, I think Mr. Seitz ought to go stuff his horse you know where. And I think the brat did good."

I was real surprised she said that, but I didn't show it. I just said, "The brat thanks you," and everybody loosened up and laughed.

I went upstairs then, to my new room. But before bed, Stephanie came in and said, real serious, "Anything you want to talk about, Sis?"

I just shook my head. I'd had enough talk.

"Anything I can help with?"

I had to smile at her, but I said, "Well, you can start doing my homework."

"C'mon." She sat on the bed by me. "How are things at school, anyway?"

"Not too bad," I told her.

Seven

SCHOOL really wasn't too bad anymore, especially after Thanksgiving vacation, when everybody started looking forward to Christmas. Everybody gets nicer around Christmas. Or maybe it was just that the kids had got tired of tormenting Shanterey and me. Anyway, things eased up, and some of my old friends started saying hi to me again. Becky was the first.

"Hi, Jenny. Hi, Shanterey."

"Hi, Becky."

Just like that, one morning in the hall. But it was important. And come to think of it, Becky never had been one to yell stuff at us or draw dirty pictures or play mean tricks. I guess less than half the kids were like that, really, once I thought about it. A lot of them just didn't have any guts. Like Becky. She was nice. I mean really nice, not like Heather. But she was chicken to go against Heather and the others.

And I would have been just like her if it hadn't been that Shan had moved right into the other half of my house and my mother had made me walk to school with her.

So things got better at school, for Shan and me both. Becky and Katie and a few of the others even started sitting with us at lunch. And we started hanging around with them at recess. Heather and her crowd didn't hang around with us, but they started letting us alone. 'Course there were some buttheaded kids who just wouldn't give up tormenting us. But we didn't pay any attention to them.

I guess Mr. Seitz would have been one of the buttheads when he was in school. He was, like, a butthead who had stayed that way when he grew up. But he had got somebody else to take care of his horse, and he and Mrs. Seitz were away visiting their son in Arizona until after Christmas, so I didn't have to worry about him. For a while.

I didn't think about Mr. Seitz or his horse too much, either, since I'd moved to the front bedroom. And Shan must have felt the same as I did, that I wanted to just forget about the horse business, because we stopped playing Wildfires for a while. We found other stuff to do. We got into my sister's makeup and we messed with each other's hair sometimes. Shan tried every way she could think of to fix my hair so it would look special for Christmas, but it always just looked like wet noodles. One time she tried to cornrow it, like hers, and she really got annoyed.

"It's, like, slimy," she complained. "It slithers. It won't stay."

"Well, it's not my fault!" I told her.

"You've got stupid hair."

"I can't help it I'm not black!"

Her hair was great, sort of soft and wiry at the same time. A person could shape it and do anything with it. I loved braiding it.

Stephanie didn't seem to mind that we got into her stuff. It must have been Christmas making her human. One Saturday she gave us a bottle of nail polish she'd only used a few times, periwinkle blue with gold flecks in it, and Shanterey and I took it over to the Lucas place and did our fingernails and toenails and Djuna's and Chelsea's fingernails, too. Then we all went for a walk to show off, the little girls, too. And we met Mrs. Raffensberger coming out her door to go shopping, and I couldn't believe it. Mrs. Raffensberger was actually sort of nice.

"You bite at your nails when you have fingernail polish on them, it'll stunt your growth," she said.

Well, that was nice for her. I mean, she was looking at Shanterey and Djuna and Chelsea same as at me when she said it. Then she asked us all what we wanted for Christmas, and she gushed over the little girls before she let us go. I guessed she was done watching the Lucases through her binoculars. It made me feel good that some people were beginning to understand. Maybe my old friends could be my friends again after all. Now if only Mr. Seitz—

"Snake," Shanterey said softly after Mrs. Raffensberger had got in her car and drove off. Even though she kept it real low, Shan's voice sounded so hard I stared at her.

"What're you talking about?" There was no snake around that I could see. The boa constrictor up the street had died the year before.

"She's a snake. One of them that'll be nice to your face and stab you in the back. I can tell."

"Oh, I don't know. . . ." I wanted to believe that Mrs. Raffensberger had really got ready to welcome black neighbors. "I mean, I used to be like that."

59

"Nuh-uh. You were never like that." Shanterey sounded real sure, about me and about Mrs. Raffensberger. I didn't argue, because maybe she was right. There was a lot to Shanterey. Taking care of her little sisters had made her sort of old in a way.

"You really want a Bible for Christmas?" I asked, because that was what she had told Mrs. Raffensberger.

"Heck, no. I was jiving her."

"What do you want, then?"

She just gave me a look down her long nose, half-teasing and half-sad, telling me I knew well enough what she wanted. And I did, too. But I couldn't give it to her, any more than her family could.

I did my best, though. And on Christmas Day I took it over—the biggest model horse I could afford, which was bigger than Stablemates but not the biggest size. A palomino, bright gold.

Shanterey didn't even act surprised when she unwrapped it. We both knew what we just had to get each other, even though Mr. Seitz had done his best to spoil horses for us.

She wasn't surprised, but her eyes lit up as she studied it. "He's different!"

"He's, like, customized," I explained to her. "I painted him some." I had painted the white star on his forehead, and the white stockings on his legs, and his clay pink hooves, and I had painted his blue-brown eyes and the pink-and-gray mottlings around his muzzle, and I had painted tiny red ribbons in his mane.

"You can do that? I didn't know you could do that!"

My horse from her was a palomino, too, a porcelain one, running.

"Wow," I said. "Thanks." It was the most beautiful horse I had.

"You're welcome."

"What's his name?"

"What do you think?"

"Bubbles? Taffy? Pumpkinhead?"

"Put that horse down so I can hit you."

But the best Christmas present we gave each other happened almost by accident.

What happened was, we were in my bedroom the day after Christmas, playing with our new Wildfires, and one of the jumps they were jumping over fell apart, and some of the poles, which were my new fruit-scented markers, rolled under the bed. So I went under after them, and while I was down there I noticed a little hole, like a mousehole, in the baseboard of the wall between my house and hers.

"Hey, Shan," I yelled out from under the

quilt, "there's a snake hole under here!" She squirmed under there next to me, and I showed her the hole and told her about the boa constrictor that had got into Mr. Runkle's house.

"No jive!" she said. "I wonder if that goes all the way through to my house."

Next thing, she was over in her room under her bed, and I was poking a coat-hanger wire through the hole, and I felt her grab hold of the other end and tug it. We pulled back and forth for a while, laughing.

"Yo, Jen!" Shan yelled. "Can you hear me?"

I could, just barely. But she couldn't hear me answer.

"Wetzel!"

I banged on the wall, and she yelled, "Never mind! Stay there. I'm coming over."

By the time she got back up to my room, I had the same idea she had. Mr. Hoffman had showed us how to do it in school. We were going to make one of those telephone sort of things out of a length of string and a couple of Styrofoam cups.

"And we'll run the string right through the hole—"

"And we can hide the cups under our beds."

"And we'll, like, talk to each other at night, once my sisters are asleep."

It would sure beat tapping on the wall at

night. I was real excited. We put the phone together in a few minutes and tried it out in the kitchen. It worked fine. We could hear each other no matter how softly we talked into the cups.

"Shan, this is gonna be great!"

"Meet you upstairs," she said, and she took her cup and the string and ran over to her place. She hooked the string to the coat-hanger wire that was still in the hole, and I pulled it through. Then I put the string back into the bottom of my own cup, pulled it tight, and said, "Hi, Shan?"

Nothing. I tapped on the wall like some prisoner in an old movie and tried again. Then she started banging on the wall like she was afraid I wasn't listening. But I was.

We weren't bothering anybody. Everybody in both our houses was out, one place or another.

Shanterey yelled to me stuff to try, like keeping the string tight or making it shorter. Half the time I couldn't understand her. We fumbled around, we tried every way we could think of to get that string phone to work through the rathole in the baseboard, but it just wouldn't. And Shan couldn't even tell if I heard her. Her voice went up high and tight.

Finally she screamed through the wall, "Oh, *crud*. I'm coming over."

By the time she got back to my house we both had it figured out from what Mr. Hoffman had told us. The string had to be straight as well as tight to vibrate the bottoms of the cups. The hole was down too low, right next to the floor. Even when we lay under the beds, we still bent the string against the top of the hole.

Shan looked as disappointed as I felt. "Crud," she said again. "I guess that's that."

I felt a crazy idea coming. "Nuh-uh," I said.

I don't think I ever would have done it if we hadn't got so close to having our phone, with both of us so excited. I felt like we couldn't give up now. I went down to the basement and got my father's electric drill. Shan's eyes widened when I came upstairs with it, holding it like a weapon. Then she smiled. A real smile, not that weird, shadowy smile of hers.

We planned where we were going to put the hole, and then she went over to make sure I didn't hit her Michael Jackson poster or her bedpost or anything.

She tapped on the wall, and I tapped back, and then I started drilling.

I was scared, because I knew that sooner or later we were going to get in trouble, and because I had never used the electric drill before, and if I slipped up and hurt myself or the wall it would be trouble sooner instead of later. But I was more excited than scared. And everything went fine. I had put in my dad's biggest, longest drill bit, and it burrowed like a carpenter bee and punched through to Shan's side of the house within a minute, and I pulled it out.

I dived under my bed, unhooked my half of the phone, got the coat-hanger wire, came up, and put it through the new hole. Shan hooked up the string, and I pulled it through. My hands were shaking; I wanted so bad for it to work. It took me a minute to hook the string up to my cup again. I pulled the phone line tight and straight—

"Shan?"

"Hi, Jen!"

"All *right!*"

"This is great! Your hole is right by my pillow."

"Mine, too. We can talk and not even have to get out of bed."

"And I can just put the cup down behind the bed and lean something up over the hole, and nobody'll ever notice. Jen?" She dropped her voice way down soft. "Can you still hear me?"

"Sure!"

"All *right!* Does your mother ever, like, clean your room or make your bed?"

"Not a chance!" We kids were supposed to take care of that stuff.

"Mine either. Jen, this is gonna be great! But we have to be careful so nobody finds out."

"Let me see something," I said, and I laid down the phone a minute and put my eye up to the hole in the wall. I could see a tiny circle of Shanterey's room. After a minute Shan's eye bobbed up in front of mine and glistened back at me, laughing like brown sunshine.

We had gone and done it. We had put a little round window in the wall.

Eight

I HUSTLED and put away the drill before anybody got home, and I cleaned up the sawdust and stuff it had left, and put the phone down behind the bed, and took my junk jewelry off my stuffed monkey, and sat him on the bed by my pillow to cover the hole and the little bit of string that showed.

Shan came over and looked and nodded, and then I went over to her place to look, and she had set up a fancy latch-hook pillow on her bed to hide the hole.

"Aunt Carmine just gave me that for Christmas," she said.

It had a picture of a horse on it, of course. "That's an ugly horse," I said.

"No duh. But it won't surprise anybody to see it on my bed all of a sudden, right?"

We went back to my place and played some stupid new game I'd got for Christmas and were real quiet with each other, and I knew both of us were thinking about later.

"You've got to wait until my sisters are sound asleep," Shan told me, and then my dad came home and started making supper and called me to help, so we couldn't say any more. Shanterey went home.

So I didn't go to bed early that night or anything like that. But when I went up, I moved my monkey and tapped on the wall, and I saw the string tighten right away. Shanterey had been waiting.

"Hi, Jen!" Real soft.

"Yo, Shan!" I kept my voice down, too.

"D'you know who I like?"

"Nuh-uh. Who?" I thought she was going to tell me about a boy.

"Michael J. Fox."

"Aw!"

"No, really! I think he's a cool dude."

"That's not what you said before. C'mon, who do you really like?"

We must have talked for hours, that night and every night during Christmas vacation.

Sometimes we didn't stop until one of us heard her parents coming up the stairs to go to bed. Something about being in the dark, late at night, lying in bed and keeping your voice low and talking with your best friend brings the secrets out. I admitted to Shan that I'd never cantered on a horse. She let me know she was scared of worms. I knew which boy in class she liked, and she knew which one I liked, and we both promised not to tell, and we didn't, either, not after we went back to school or anytime.

When we went back to school, we stopped talking so late at night, but we still talked for a few minutes or maybe an hour just about every night before we went to sleep. A lot of the time we talked about horses.

"Hey, Shan! Maybe we could get our folks to put both our backyards together and put up a fence, and we could buy Wildfire from Mr. Seitz and keep him there."

"Right, Jen." We both knew it wasn't going to happen. "What you using for money?"

"We could get paper routes."

"We're not old enough for paper routes."

"Well, when we get older, then. Wouldn't it be great to have Wildfire?" The backyards weren't big enough, not really.

Shan said, "It would be great to have *any* Wildfire."

"If there was any other horse around here, Shan, I'd know about it."

"No duh." She knew as well as I did that if there was another horse within biking distance I would have found it and tried to make friends with it. After a little while she said, "Jen—what was it like to ride Wildfire?"

I heard the ache in her voice and didn't know how to answer her. I just lay there.

She wouldn't give up. "Was he nice?"

"Yeah." Riding Wildfire—what else could I say? "It was good." I was wishing she could see for herself, and that made me think of why she couldn't, and that made me think of the bad news. "Guess what I found out at supper tonight, Shan?"

"What?"

"Mr. Seitz is back."

"Great." She sounded disgusted. "Just what I needed to know."

She wasn't likely to run into him anywhere, but she might. In the drugstore or someplace. And things were getting bad at school again. All through January school had been okay, with just a few real butthead kids hassling and tormenting Shan and me. But by February almost everybody was turning into a butthead. It was the cold, gloomy time of year, with nothing but school, school, school every week and no relief in sight until Easter. A lot of kids started to feel mean and took it out on whoever was handy. And Shanterey was handiest of all.

During the winter we mostly had gym class inside, and a lot of the time we played basketball. Just because she was tall, everyone thought Shan would be good at basketball, but she wasn't. She hated being tall. Whenever people looked at her because she was tall, she got slouchy and awkward. And whenever anybody passed her the basketball, she froze and dropped it or tripped over her own feet or something. Even when she shot at the basket, she almost always missed.

"Pass it, nigger!" one of the boys on her team yelled at her one day. "Jeez, you don't even make a proper nigger! Don't play basketball!"

"Or dance or anything!" one of the girls put in.

Mr. Hoffman wouldn't have allowed that sort of talk, but Mr. Ruth, the phys ed teacher, pretended not to hear. The rest of the game, people laughed and talked about how Shanterey didn't do the things blacks were supposed to do, like talk bad grammar and eat lots of soul food.

Shanterey acted the same as usual on the way home and when I talked to her on our private line at bedtime. I went to sleep. But sometime in the middle of the night something woke me up. I really sleep when I'm sleeping, and it took a while. When I finally came awake, I knew the noise had been going on for some time.

Tap. Tap. Tap. Sort of slow, as if she had about given up. Shanterey was tapping on the wall.

I grabbed for the string and fished my Styrofoam cup out from behind the bed.

"Shan?"

"Jen. Uh, I couldn't sleep." Something shaky in Shanterey's voice.

"What's wrong?"

"It's just . . ." I knew from her voice that she had been crying. That she was still crying. "Jen, what's the use?" she burst out. "I don't fit in anywhere."

"Shhhh." I meant it like, don't cry, but maybe she took it that she was making too much noise. She lowered her voice. Her words sounded as if they were coming out between clenched teeth.

"Where we lived before, I didn't fit in, either. People said I was an Oreo. Only black on the outside. Too much like a white person. And here, they can't think of anything 'cept that I'm black!"

I guess I should have known that people's meanness bothered her more than she showed.

She said, "Sometimes I feel like just giving up."

"No," I said. "Shh. Shan. Listen. You fit in with me, don't you? And with your family and stuff, and my family?"

"It's not the same. You know what I mean."

I swallowed hard, because I knew what she meant all right. It's not easy being picked on in school. And not belonging, not being one of the group, not having a lot of friends—I was just beginning to know how rough it was.

Then I thought of something that might help her. It would mean trouble, because grown-ups wouldn't understand. But I understood a few things. I knew Shan couldn't fit in—no way in my town—but if she could at least feel big inside, feel like life was good . . . and I knew what made me feel like I could lick the world. What would make her feel that way. What she needed, just like a person needs food when they're hungry.

"You're gonna ride Wildfire," I told her.

It was like I was still dreaming even though Shan had woke me up, or I probably wouldn't have said it. But I did say it. And I knew as soon as I said it that I was crazy.

A little quiet space. Then Shan said, "Wetzel, what the heck you talking about?"

Just the way she said Wetzel, I knew I'd managed to change her mood, and that clinched it. I couldn't take back what I'd said. I had to do it for her somehow.

"You're gonna ride Wildfire," I promised. "We'll do it some way. Now go to sleep, wouldja?"

"You're a goof."

"So are you. G'night."

I hoped she went to sleep, but I didn't. Not right away. I was thinking, and I was worried. Getting Shan to that horse was going to be risky.

If I'd been thinking about Mr. Seitz, instead of just about getting in trouble with our parents, I would have been more than worried. I would have been scared. But I wasn't thinking about Mr. Seitz. Or I was still thinking of him the way I'd known him since I was a little kid. Even after the way he was with Shan, I still couldn't believe he'd ever do anything really mean.

Maybe Shan had more idea than I did what he was really like, because when I saw her the next day, walking to school, she started right up where we'd left off.

"You goof! You're crazy."

"So are you. I should know." She was the nicest crazy person I knew. A girl who named all her horses Wildfire.

"Jen, c'mon, be serious." She sunk her voice down so her sisters wouldn't hear us. "We can't—you know."

"We can, too!" I sort of shouted between my teeth, trying to keep my voice low. "It's not fair unless we do."

What Mr. Seitz had done to Shan was wrong, and I knew she would feel better when we had made it right. Sort of. As best we could.

"We can do it," I said like somebody in the movies about to fight the Mafia. "We can do it." Shan and me together. And she looked at me with that strange, quiet smile of hers.

"Okay," she said, and that settled it. And I knew it was going to be worth whatever happened, because she didn't look like a person who wanted to give up on herself anymore. She looked like a person who was going to ride Wildfire.

We talked it over the next few nights at bedtime and worked out a strategy. It was no use talking to Mr. Seitz. We wished it would have been that simple, but we knew better. So we were going to have to wait for a day when he was gone, and Mrs. Seitz was gone, and my family and Shan's family, too, since they all knew now how he felt about Shan and his horse. A Sunday morning, probably. We thought about skipping school, but Mrs. Seitz would probably be home on a school day.

A Sunday morning with nobody around. The rest of February and all of March went by before it happened. My folks usually hung around, lay in bed, and read the paper on Sunday mornings, and Stephanie usually played her boom box and looked out that back window of hers.

The second weekend in April, though, Stephanie was gone all weekend on a school trip and Mom and Dad had a class reunion covered-dish dinner to go to way over in Lancaster. I asked if I could stay home, because I would be bored, and they said okay.

With all the time that had gone by, it seemed like a dream that Shan and I were really going to do what we had promised we would. Not that we had changed our minds or anything, but it didn't seem real. I talked it over with Shan one last time Saturday night on our private line, and it still didn't seem like I was awake. I know why, now. We were going to do something that would change us both. That would change our lives. No wonder everything seemed new and strange.

Shan had her part of the plan under control. Her whole family would head toward church and dinner back in Harrisburg, the way they always did on Sunday. Shan had already picked at her supper and gone to bed early. She would play sick, but not so sick that anybody would have to stay with her.

"Make sure you stay in bed five minutes after they leave, just in case they come back for something they forgot," I told her.

"Right, Wetzel."

"There won't be any hurry. We'll have to wait for Seitzes to go to church."

"I hear you, Jen! Go to sleep."

I couldn't sleep. It all had to work out. . . .

It did. My folks left early, before I was up. Shan's mother did come back for something she forgot, and Shan was still in bed. Three minutes later, though, she was dressed and over at my place, and we were both up in Steph's room, lying on her bed with our heads at the window, waiting for Mr. and Mrs. Seitz to leave. It seemed like forever before the blue Buick pulled out of their lane. When it finally did, we both jumped up, but then Shanterey froze.

"How do we know they're both in the car?"

77

"Mrs. Seitz hardly ever drives. And Mr. Seitz wouldn't go to church by himself. She's the one who makes him go."

"Yeah, but . . ." Shanterey was having cold feet.

"Come on, Shan!"

She smiled that weird smile of hers and unfroze, and we ran out through the dewy grass, down the yard, and over the fence into the pasture. It was a wonderful day, cool and soft and sunny, with the smell of hyacinth in it. There were birds in the sky and daffodils growing wild in the pasture.

And there was Wildfire, prancing, with the yellow flowers making lights on his flame gold sides.

I ran to the barn for the halter.

It wasn't easy for us to catch Wildfire. He acted like spring had made him crazy. He threw up his head and hightailed it with his white mane flying, and when we tried to corner him, he dodged us and went skittering through the new grass. But Shan and I followed and coaxed, and he finally let us come up to him.

We didn't have to lead him to a fence. I gave Shan a boost, and she was on and riding Wildfire.

I watched—it was worth all the risk just to watch her ride up through the green and yellow to the hillcrest. Tall, she sat tall on Wildfire, with her head up and her back straight, and her legs stretched down his sides, and when he ran she faced the wind, and her shoulders swung with his strides. And the sun on them both—it was beautiful. And she made Wildfire canter and canter, and she made him jump the barrier I had set up months before. I think she could have made him jump the pasture fence. She could have ridden him away from that town into wherever. I think she and that horse could have done anything.

"Wow," I said, when she finally rode up to me and made Wildfire stop. "Shan, don't ever tell me you don't belong anywhere. You belong on that horse."

Then I looked at her face, and there were tears down her cheeks, one on each, shining on her brown skin like racing stripes. Whipped out of her by the wind, maybe.

She said, "You want to ride? He'll canter for you today."

I shook my head. "It's your day to ride."

Then she was away again. She rode like she was part of the horse. Her long legs hugged him the way my stumpy ones never did. Her hands were strong. When she stopped Wildfire at the top of the hill, she looked around her, then laid her head down on his mane and hugged him around his neck.

79

The morning wasn't nearly long enough. And neither of us had a watch, but after a while Shan and I looked at each other and nodded. It was time to go.

When I came back to the pasture from taking the halter down to the barn, I found Shan just standing there, looking at Wildfire.

She said, "When I was up on him, it was like I could see forever."

I told her, "You were born to ride horses."

"What's the good of that, if people won't let me?"

Her shoulders slumped. The sight of that hurt me worse than if she had cried.

"Shan . . ." I didn't know what to say to her.

She said in a dead voice, "I'll never have a horse of my own. I'm down on the ground now, and the world's gonna keep me in my place."

We walked toward home. I wished I could argue with her, that things could go better, that it didn't always have to be bad things happening to her. But I had a sick feeling. I had seen something move in a window three houses up the street. Old Mrs. Raffensberger had been watching us.

Nine

THURSDAY the next week, around supper-time, I was over at Lucases' when the township cop knocked at the door and handed Mrs. Lucas a summons. It was for juvenile court, made out against Shanterey Lucas, by Wilmer Seitz, for trespassing.

It's a good thing I was there, because Shan would've tried to get through it without telling anybody I was on Mr. Seitz's land with her. As it was, we were both in trouble together.

"We were both on his land," I pointed out to Mr. and Mrs. Lucas. "Why doesn't he get me for trespassing?"

Mr. Lucas said, "He allowed you on his horse and his land! Shanterey he didn't allow."

"And that's not fair."

"It's not fair, but it's the law that he can let on his property who he wants and keep off who he wants. And, by God, in this family we obey the law!" He wasn't really shouting, compared to most people, but for Mr. Lucas it was shouting. "One of my children in trouble with the law! I can't believe it." He glared, at Shan more than me, but at me some. "What the heck possessed you? Why'd you do it?"

Shanterey didn't seem to have an answer. They were her own parents, after all. They might kill her if she talked back, but I figured they wouldn't kill me, and I said, "Shan had to ride Wildfire."

"What sort of—"

I interrupted Mr. Lucas. "She had to. You should have seen her." I tried to make him understand how beautiful it was. "She sat straight, her head was up. She sat tall."

As if I had reminded her of something, Shanterey lifted her chin, straightened her spine, and looked her parents in their faces. She didn't say anything. And what I had said wasn't nearly enough to make them really understand. But they must have had some idea, because Mrs. Lucas sort of nodded, and when Mr. Lucas started talking again his voice was softer.

"All right. What's done is done. The main thing is, what do we do now? We can't afford some hotshot lawyer."

"Not much we can do except hope for a good judge," said Mrs. Lucas. "Jennifer, you go on home."

I told her, "I can't just go on home and leave Shan when I got her into this."

"You're gonna have to when she goes to court," Mrs. Lucas said, sort of grim. "You're not invited. Go on, now."

"It's all right, Jen," Shan said, and she sounded strong, the way she had been strong the day she rode Wildfire, and I knew I would talk to her at bedtime. So I went.

Stephanie wasn't home, because she was spending the night with a friend. But my mom and dad were both in the kitchen, and supper was just about ready. And I didn't feel hungry. I guess I could have kept quiet and they might not have heard about what Shan and I had done for a while, but I couldn't stand it. I burst out, "Mom. Dad. I need help."

They turned and looked at me, and then they both just left the food on the stove, sat down on the kitchen chairs, and looked at me. And the more I told them about what had happened, the worse they looked.

"Stupid," was all my dad said when I was done, because I guess he knew I felt bad enough. "Jennifer, that was just plain stupid."

"I was just trying to do what was fair."

"Some things in life aren't fair! Is lightning fair when it hits you? Is it smart to run out in a storm and yell at it to be fair? Huh!" My dad got up, pulled his jacket off a chair back, and put it on, stomping. He said to my mother, "I'm going down to talk to Seitz."

"Is this the man who doesn't like trouble with the neighbors?" Mom sounded half-teasing, half-proud. "Do you want me to do it?"

"He'll listen better to me." She gave him a look, and he added, "I'm not a sexist, woman, but he probably is. Don't wait supper for me." He went out.

Mom looked at me. "You want supper?"

I shook my head. Supper could sit on the stove.

Mom eyed me hard and said, "Poor Shanterey. I bet they're giving her what for. It's no wonder you feel bad, Jennifer Kay. Dragging her into this mess." Which I sort of had. Mom knew me too well. "I'm going over there," she said. "See how things are going."

She went out, and after a minute I trailed after her.

84

Lucases weren't giving Shanterey what for, not really. They were just sitting around, the whole bunch of them except Djuna and Chelsea, talking and looking worried. Mom and I sat down with them, and we did more of the same. So there we all were, and in an hour we hadn't managed to do anything but decide Mrs. Raffensberger must have told Mr. Seitz, when my dad knocked and came in.

Mom looked at him with her eyebrows up, asking a silent question. She hadn't told the Lucases where he was. Didn't want to get their hopes up, I guess. And I had kept my mouth shut, too. I was in enough trouble for one day.

Dad just shrugged at Mom. One of the Lucas boys—Dwayne, I think it was—got up to give him a chair, and he flapped one hand in the air as he sat down in it. He said to Mom, "Mrs. Seitz is on our side, more or less. She doesn't approve of Shanterey—" Dad smiled at Shan. "—but she doesn't want to go to court, either. But old man Seitz is Dutch."

Stubborn, that meant.

Mr. and Mrs. Lucas looked at each other, and then Mrs. Lucas said to Dad, "We appreciate what you tried to do."

"Oh, I ain't done yet." Dad leaned back in his chair and sort of showed his teeth. "I'm

Dutch, too, and I got a few things to try yet. Mr. Seitz is a churchgoer. I'm going to get his preacher out to talk to him, for starters."

That didn't sound too hopeful to me, and I noticed nobody else exactly jumped up and danced, either. A little bit later, we Wetzels got up and went home. I went straight to bed, and I wasn't surprised to find Shan up in her room already. When I tapped, she picked up the phone right away.

"Shan, you all right?"

"Wetzel," she said, and she chuckled into the phone, real low, and that's all she said.

"Well, I can't help it! I feel bad. It was my idea."

"I have a mouth to say no. I didn't have to go. Anyway . . ." Shanterey lowered her voice even more. "It was worth it."

I felt a warm glow, as if the sunshine of that day was still touching me, and I nodded in the dark. "Yeah," I said.

There was a silence, and I guess we were both thinking of Wildfire.

"So your parents aren't too mad?" I asked Shan after a while.

"No. They're worried, but I think they sort of understand." The chuckle came back into her voice as she added, "Even if they didn't, they don't beat me, Jen, for crying out loud. So calm down."

"Are you grounded, anything like that?"

"No. I'm just supposed to stay away from Seitz. You?"

"Same."

We didn't say anything for a while, and then Shan said, almost in a whisper, "Someday I'm going to have a horse like that. So what if I have to get a job blacks don't have and live in a place blacks don't live? So what if I'm old and gray? I'm going to have my own horse someday."

I nodded as if she could see me, and we were quiet. Then I said, "Hey, Shan, what are you going to name it?"

"Remind me to hit you in the morning, Chenny."

"Sure, Shan."

"Go to sleep, Wetzel."

Actually, she was kind of quiet in the morning. And school wasn't any better than usual, for either of us. So we were, like, worn out on the way home and just went to our houses without saying much.

I was surprised to find Dad home. He had taken the day off from work. He asked me how school was and everything, like he was worried about me, and he was so nice he almost made me cry. When things are going wrong, I can take anything but niceness.

Supper was pretty awful. It was what we were supposed to have had the night before, warmed up, and spanish rice doesn't warm up very well if you don't have a microwave. But nobody complained, not even Stephanie, which sort of made it worse.

After supper Dad went out, and Mom and Steph and I went over to Lucases' to see how they were doing.

We sat around and talked about anything except what everybody was thinking about. And after a little while Dad came in. He didn't look at Mom, and he didn't smile. But he said to Mr. and Mrs. Lucas, "Seitz is going to drop the trespassing charge."

All the kids started talking, because we were surprised, but the grown-ups just looked back at him, not saying anything. I was the only one who yelled, "All right!"

Shanterey said, quiet, "You went down and talked with him again, Mr. Wetzel?"

"Right." Dad sat down. He looked tired, the way I had felt after school.

I was beginning to see what the problem was. It must not have been an easy talk. I lowered my voice to ask Dad, "What made him change his mind?"

"He hasn't had a change of heart, if that's what you're hoping, young lady." Dad gave me a sour look. "I told him I'd bad-mouth him to everybody in the county, is all. And set all the preachers on him. And I threatened him with a lawsuit for what he said to your mother that time. And reminded him that he doesn't have a case, because no daughter of mine was going to testify."

My mouth came open and felt around at the air. Dad started to grin, then turned his eyes away from me to stop himself, because the Lucases were still looking worried.

"I went and talked to the magistrate today," he explained to them. "Old man Seitz needs two kinds of witnesses. One that Shanterey was on his land, which he's got. And one that Shanterey was told to stay off his land. Jenny is the only witness who ever heard him say that to her."

They stirred and nodded. "We're grateful," Mrs. Lucas said.

"Don't be." Dad sighed. "Nothing's changed, really. Except I guess Seitz is madder than ever."

"We'll stay out of his way," Mr. Lucas said. "Shanterey?"

She looked at her father and nodded, then looked at my father and said, "Thank you." And she meant it.

My family went home, and when I went to bed I slept better than I had the night before, because I figured things were getting better. But they weren't. Shan and I hadn't meant to, but we had started something that just wasn't going to stop.

The next morning, when Stephanie went outside to go to school, she hollered, "Mom!" And something in her voice made us all come out to see.

There were words written big on the house, our side and Lucases' side, too. Right on the front, in white spray paint. "Nigger house." And there were words spray-painted on the sidewalk and on the street, and on our cars: "Nigger lovers" and "Niggers go back to the jungle" and a lot of other things I can't repeat.

Ten

WHITE spray paint on the house, white chalk on the playground, it's all part of the same thing. My guess is whoever had written on our house— we couldn't say for sure it was Mr. Seitz or any one person—the buttheads who had done it got their training on a playground somewhere.

Things at school got ugly. A person would think that kids would feel good in the springtime, but they don't. Maybe the sun comes out and all the flowers are blooming and the air smells sweet, but instead of getting nice, kids just sort of go nuts. They want to be out of school, and wanting makes them mean.

Or maybe some of them were hearing the

grown-up buttheads talking about Shan and me, and it gave them ideas. Rumors started going around that we were gay. Some of the kids who had been friends with us during the winter turned against us again.

"Nigger queer!"

"Hey, here come the nigger and the nigger lover!"

"Fags!"

I didn't know what they were talking about, and I bet a lot of them didn't, either. But I knew I didn't like it.

"Never mind, Shan," I told her. "Pretty soon school will be out and we'll have the summer to ourselves."

But she did mind. I didn't know how much, though, till almost the end of school.

It was recess, and Shan and I had gone to the far end of the playground, where there were fewer kids to bother us, when Becky came running up to us. She was one who had stayed friends with us, kind of. She was chicken in some ways, didn't like to stand up to the other kids, but she didn't like meanness. "They're scaring your sisters," she puffed at Shan. "Around front."

Shan took off, and I ran along behind her. I never could keep up with her, running. She swerved around the corner of the school way ahead of me, and when I got to where I could see what was happening, she was already in action.

Some of the big kids had invaded the front playground where the little kids go. I don't know what they had said or done, but Djuna and Chelsea were holding onto each other and crying. And I don't think Shan had stopped to ask questions. She had jumped about three fifth-grade boys at once, and the rest of the big kids were jumping her. Including Heather, of course.

I piled in, pulled Heather off Shan's back by her long, permed hair, swung her around, and sent her flying. Then I think I rammed one of the boys with my head. After that, I don't remember much of what I did, but I remember Shanterey, how she fought. She had her head up, and she was taller than anybody else there, and she hit with hard fists on those long arms of hers, and nobody could get near her. And she didn't yell or anything; she was so cool, like somebody in a movie. I think she could have taken on the whole mob of them by herself. When she really got moving, I think she could take on the world.

Then Mr. Hoffman was there, breaking it up before the two of us could really lick the bunch of them. Shanterey didn't even look at him. She went to her sisters, crouched down, and put her arms around them and whispered to them until they stopped crying.

Mr. Hoffman was busy rounding up the

other kids. Then he herded us all inside to see the principal.

He put Shan and me in a separate room from the others. Shan didn't have a mark on her that I could see, but I had a messed-up face and a bloody nose. Mr. Hoffman handed me a wad of Kleenex for my nose, then went to get ice or the nurse or something.

"Wow," I said to Shanterey as soon as he was out of the room. "Being tall is good for some things, Shan."

She didn't look at me. She just said, sort of panicky, "We're going to get paddled."

That scared me. "You really think so?"

She looked at me then, because my voice came out funny from under the Kleenex. "I mean, I'm going to get paddled," she said. "Because I'm black."

"Shan, that stinks!"

She looked down at her hands, curled like fists in her lap. "And I'm going to get in trouble at home, for fighting. I'm not supposed to fight."

I didn't get a chance to say any more to her, because Mr. Hoffman came back in with a bag of ice and a wet paper towel. He handed me the ice and started dabbing at me with the towel. But he looked at Shan. "Shanterey. You okay?"

She said to him in the same sort of panicky

94

way, "They better let my sisters alone. They can say anything they want to to me, but they better not mess with my sisters."

"I checked on your sisters. They're fine."

"Mr. Hoffman," I blurted out, "Shan says she's going to get paddled because she's black."

He sort of winced, and he said, "Shanterey, I hope it's not like that here. Just calm down before you go see Mrs. Paules. Okay? Jennifer, you okay?"

What did he mean, was I okay, when I was sitting there with a bloody nose? But I said, "Sure."

The principal didn't paddle anybody. I knew as soon as I saw her that she was fussed, but not at me and Shan exactly. I didn't know what Mrs. Paules was like, none of us saw her much because she had more than one school to be at, but I could tell she wasn't a mean person. I even started to hope she could help Shan somehow.

She told me and Shan to sit down, and she said right away to Shan, looking at her straight, "I don't like to believe we have a situation of racism here. I can't understand why we should."

Shan just looked back at her, and after a minute Mrs. Paules went on talking. "I've been at several schools that had minority students and no such difficulties. It seems to me, Shanterey, that if you made a little more effort to fit in, to be pleasant to the other children—"

Shan burst out, "Is it right they should hassle me when I don't do anything to them?"

"No, it's not. But I'm sure you're not the only child who is teased."

I knew what Mrs. Paules meant. Lots of kids were picked on, because they were too skinny or too fat or too smart or too dumb or whatever. Probably Shan would have been picked on even if she was white, just because she was so tall and quiet. Thing was, if Shan was a different sort of person, maybe she would have got along. But— something wasn't right about what Mrs. Paules was saying. I couldn't put my finger on it, but I knew one thing for sure: Mrs. Paules wasn't going to be any help to us. She meant to be, but she wasn't.

Shan said, "So kids are mean to other kids besides me and my sisters. That makes it okay?" She sure wasn't scared of Mrs. Paules anymore. Maybe Mrs. Paules couldn't see her clenched fists, but we both could see the set of her jaw. Shan was mad clear to her bones. And she was sitting tall.

Maybe Mrs. Paules had sort of helped after all, but not the way she meant.

That was the thing about Shan: pride. She was quiet, didn't say much, but she didn't give

96

in to buttheads. Not by crying or talking back or smiling or trying to be friends or shouting that she hated them or anything. That's why they just kept coming after her and coming after her and coming after her. I knew what was wrong with Mrs. Paules: She didn't understand pride in a kid.

She sighed, and gave up talking at us, and told us fighting wasn't allowed, and gave us detention, same as the others. It could have been worse.

Shan didn't get in much trouble at home, either, because her parents had other things to think about. Both her brothers had got in fights at the high school that same day. Stephanie told us about it at supper. And somebody had slashed Mrs. Lucas's tires while she was at work. All four of them.

Could have been worse, huh. It was worse. Bad things were happening.

That night, for the first time since we had put it in, Shan didn't talk on our private phone. Not at all. And all the Lucas kids stayed home from school the next day. I went anyway. Mom took me. The kids I had fought with just sort of kept away from me, because Mr. Hoffman had given them a talking-to, but I knew that wouldn't last. And I kept worrying what was wrong with Shan.

After school I went over to her place to ask her what was going on, was she real sick or mad at me or what, and little Djuna met me at the door. "We're moving!" she sang out.

"Shhh." Quinn pulled her back inside. "C'mon in, Jen."

Shan was up in her room, sitting on her bed, and she started crying when she saw me.

It turned out she didn't know how to tell me—that was why she hadn't been talking to me. The reason they were moving was there had been a lot of threats, stuff I didn't know about. Mr. and Mrs. Lucas had decided to give it up. They were taking the family back to Harrisburg, where they had lived before.

I hugged Shan and told her we could still be friends, even though it wouldn't be the same, and I would miss her. It didn't really hit me till I got home how much I would miss her. Then I started crying myself.

We talked on our phone that night. Not about anything in particular, but we talked late anyway, because soon we wouldn't be able to. Lucases were going to move as fast as they could manage it, maybe the next weekend. The kids were going to stay home and pack in the daytime, since the buttheaded bigots wouldn't let them learn at school.

I thought things had sort of hit bottom, that they'd got as bad as they could possibly get, but I was wrong. I still had to learn how sick people could be.

I learned the next morning, when I saw what had happened during the night.

Stephanie didn't even holler when she found it. She just came back into the kitchen with her face white, and we went out to look. Mr. Seitz's palomino horse was lying in front of our house, across both sidewalks. Dead, with its throat cut.

And words spray-painted on it, right on the golden hide: "Here's your horse, nigger girl."

Shanterey didn't cry when she saw—not Wildfire, I didn't want to call the dead thing Wildfire—she didn't cry when she saw the horse. She didn't even say anything. But her face went dead, and she stood like wood while everybody else ran to keep the little girls away or call the cops or clean up the blood.

I guess the cops got somebody with a hoist to come take the horse away. I guess they took it to the dump or something. I don't know. I was in school, and all day I couldn't seem to think straight or talk straight or anything. Anyway, when I got home, it was gone.

Right away I went over to see Shan. She

didn't look up at me or say hi to me when I came in her room. And all the model horses were gone off her dresser.

"Where are all the Wildfires?" I asked her. They were the first thing she had unpacked. They should have been the last thing she packed.

She wouldn't look at me. She wouldn't even talk to me at first. I kept asking, and finally she said, "I buried them."

"Huh?"

She said like some sort of machine or robot, still not looking at me, "I wrapped them in tissue paper and put them in boxes and buried them out back. In a big grave."

I stared at her for a minute. Then I went home and got all my own toy horses and model horses and china horses out of my bedroom, all except the one she had given me for Christmas. That one I kept. But all the rest of them I took in my arms over to Shan's house and up to her bedroom.

"Okay," I told her, "those Wildfires are dead, but these ones are still alive. Take 'em."

She looked at me then. I guess she didn't believe me. But I shoved her until she sat down on her bed, and then I piled all the little horses in her lap.

"You take them," I ordered her, "and you keep them, or I'm coming after you." Then, before she could say anything, I asked her, "Why are they all named Wildfire, anyway?"

She was looking up at me, and her face came back to life, and she smiled, that secret smile of hers. And by then I was beginning to understand it.

"Jen," she said, "it's, like, a feeling I get. That they can all be beautiful, and all be free."

"Yeah," I said.

I sat down beside her. We just sat there for a while without saying anything.

Then I said, real soft, "People, too? Someday? Maybe?"

It was a long time before she answered. But finally she said, just as soft, "Maybe."

That night we talked on our phone for the last time and made each other some promises, then pulled it out of the wall.

The next day, Saturday, all us Wetzels went over to help the Lucases move. It felt wrong, them moving at all, but we felt like the least we could do was help them load their stuff.

About noontime, I guess it was, Mr. Lucas called my dad inside, and then Mrs. Lucas motioned out a window at my mom to come see something. Shanterey and I didn't pay much at-

101

RETA E. KING LIBRARY
CHADRON STATE COLLEGE
CHADRON, NE 69337

tention at first. We were both kind of numb. But after a few minutes we began to get curious, and we went in, too.

The beds were out of the front bedroom, and the four adults were standing in there, looking at the tiny round hole Shan and I had made in the wall with no windows.

I grabbed at Shan's hand and found it already halfway to mine. It sounds stupid, but that's the way it was. Then my dad looked over and saw us standing there holding onto each other.

"You girls can let go," he said, real gentle. "We aren't going to yell at you. Who made the hole?"

I swallowed. "I did."

"With my drill. I wondered what the heck happened to that bit."

Shan said, "We both did it together."

Mrs. Lucas said, just as gentle as my dad, "You two were talking to each other? After bedtime, maybe?"

We just nodded. I didn't feel up to explaining about the Styrofoam cups and string.

"Well, I'll be," my dad muttered.

My mom came over and touched my hair, then went on past me. "I'll get the patching plaster and fill it up," she said. "Otherwise, the next people are going to think it's a peephole."

That sort of hit me. The next people. I made up my mind I was going to hate them.

We finished loading the truck, and Shan hugged me once, quick, and got in the car. Us Wetzels stood around, awkward, while the Lucases split up between their car and the U-Haul.

"You got your Wildfires?" I said to Shan.

"Right here." She patted a big box at her feet, and she gave me her dreaming smile. "I'll always have them."

That was all I could do, except wave at her as they drove away.

So that was that. Shan and I said we would call each other and write, but you know how that goes. We were friends, but after a person moves away, it's never the same again.

The spray paint and threats and stuff stopped after the Lucases went away. New people moved in next door, and I didn't hate them after all. By the end of summer, Mrs. Raffensberger and Mr. Seitz both acted the same as they ever did, and we acted the same to them, because Dad didn't like trouble with the neighbors. In the fall, the kids at school got to be friends with me again, for the most part. Nobody talked about Shanterey.

Nothing seemed to have changed.

Except, I guess, me.